Blade, Adam.
Gryph, the feathered
Fiend /
2016.
33305236615898
ca   08/08/16

Quest®

GrypH
THE FEATHERED
FIEND

BY ADAM BLADE

ORCHARD

VAREEN

THE ICE
CASTLE

THE ICY PLAINS

FREESHOR

CITY OF
JENGTOR

GWILDOR BORDERLANDS

PORTAL

MUDDY LAKE

MANGROVE SWAMP

DUNES

DESERT

CONTENTS

Do you know the worst thing about so-called heroes? They just don't give up.

Well, villains can be just as stubborn... That pesky boy, Tom, and his lackey, Elenna, may have thwarted our siege of Jengtor, but the battle is not over. There are other prizes to be found throughout my kingdom!

In Gwildor's borderlands lie the four pieces of the Broken Star, a legendary "gift" that fell from the sky many, many years ago. Each piece gives its holder immense power, and whoever brings all four pieces together will be undefeatable!

To obtain each piece, one must find a way past the Beasts which guard them. Kensa and I have tricks up our sleeves – and a head-start on our enemies. With the star in our hands, no one will stop us from reclaiming Gwildor.

And then? Avantia!

Your future ruler,

Emperor Jeng

SANPAO'S WEAKNESS

Tom's boots rang hollowly on
the stone steps as he and Elenna
climbed down into the gloom
beneath the Palace of Jengtor. Tom
clenched his fists as he followed
the spiral stairs, trying to keep
his anger in check. He'd put off
this meeting for as long as he

could – ever since he and Elenna
had freed the city from the Pirate
King Sanpao. But now they needed
information, and they needed it
quickly.

Tom's torch cast flickering shadows onto the circular stairwell walls. But its acrid smoke did little to mask the stench rising to meet them – the musty reek of rats, decay and sweat.

The staircase led them down into a narrow passage lined with doorways barred with iron. From the shadows beyond the first door, Tom could hear the slow, regular hiss of breathing. He slid a heavy key from his pocket, opened the cell with an echoing clank, and stepped inside.

The light from Tom's torch licked across damp, crumbling brickwork. Dark eyes glinted back at him from the corner. Sanpao. The barrel-chested pirate was slumped in the shadows, chained by manacles to the wall. His greasy hair hung limply over his ears. Sanpao had once been known for his long, oiled ponytail – until Tom's blade sliced it off in the battle of Jengtor.

The pirate king squinted into the torchlight, then scowled. "Come to gloat, have you?" he said.

Tom heard the scuff of Elenna's boots as she entered the cell behind him. "We've come for information," she said.

Tom stepped towards the hunched pirate. "You know what Kensa and Jeng are planning," he said. "Now's the time to talk."

Sanpao looked up at Tom, his eyes wide with mock surprise. "Oh?" he said. "So, if I spill my guts you'll let me go, will you?"

Tom glared scornfully back at the pirate.

Sanpao turned his head and spat. "No. I didn't think so. So if you don't mind closing the door behind you, I'll get back to my nap." The pirate settled himself against the slimy wall, his legs crossed at the ankles and his chin on his chest.

Tom thrust his torch close to the pirate's face. "I could *make* you talk!" he said.

Sanpao opened his eyes lazily,

then let out a short bark of laugher.
"You?" he said. "I've commanded the
most ruthless bunch of bloodthirsty

cut-throats in all the known kingdoms. There's nothing you and that scrawny lass could do that would even tickle me."

"Is that right?" Tom said, balling his fist. "If I call on the strength of my golden breastplate, I could punch you straight through that wall!"

Sanpao grinned. "Now you're talking!" he said. "It's about time I got out of this stinking latrine. I'm not fussy about using the door."

Tom closed his eyes and let his breath out slowly, forcing himself to relax. *I have to play this right...* he told himself. *The fate of Gwildor depends on it.* But it was so hard not to just wipe the smirk off Sanpao's face with his fist. The blood pounded in Tom's ears. He couldn't stop thinking about the sickness and pain his mother had been through – all because of Sanpao's evil greed. Tom felt a gentle touch on his arm, and Elenna stepped past him. She stopped before Sanpao, and ran a cool gaze over the pirate's lank hair and filthy clothes.

"You know something, Sanpao?" Elenna said. "Even if you did get out of here, you'd never catch up with Kensa. She chose Jeng over you." Elenna shrugged. "And why wouldn't she? You're just the so-called 'king' of a grubby little pirate ship with more woodworm than worthy crew. But

Jeng…" Elenna spread her arms wide.
"*He* can offer her a whole realm."

Tom saw Sanpao's broad chest
heave. The muscles in the pirate's
jaw tensed, and he sat up straight.
"That stuck-up, snot-nosed swindler,"
Sanpao growled. "He can't very well
give Kensa a realm if someone takes
it off him first, can he?" Sanpao
cracked his knuckles. Then he craned
forwards and tapped his nose. "Which
is what's going to happen, because
I know what he's after!" The pirate's
face spread into an ugly, black-
toothed leer. "Some lousy star up in
the North, that's what."

Good work, Elenna! Tom stifled
the urge to grin. "We can make sure

he fails," Tom said, "if you just tell us what he has planned."

Sanpao sat back. His shoulders sagged. "They never told me the details. But I do know they're after something pretty powerful." Sanpao smashed his fist down against the stone floor. "We were supposed to go together!" He slumped down again and glanced sulkily up at Tom. "You know what? All this talking makes a man's throat rather dry," he said. "That information wouldn't be worth a few sips of ale, would it?"

Tom swallowed his hatred and revulsion for the pirate, and nodded. "I'll ask Irina to get you some water," he said. Then he turned on his heel and led Elenna out of the cell.

Back on the stairway to the gilded passages above, Tom shot Elenna a grin. "You're a genius!" he said. "You knew just what to say to Sanpao."

Elenna shrugged. "No matter how tough that big brute acts, Kensa will always be his weak spot."

"Just as well for us," Tom said. "Hopefully Irina will know more about that 'star'…" Tom stopped suddenly, a familiar tingling warmth coming from his belt. He glanced down to see his red jewel glowing brightly.

"Trouble?" Elenna asked. Tom put his hand to the jewel and closed his eyes. He caught the sound of a distant cry, almost drowned out by buffeting

wind. It was a voice he recognised.
"Koldo the Arctic Warrior," Tom
said. He focused hard, trying to hear
the Good Beast's words. *Tom*, the

voice called to him. *You must come to Freeshor. Evil intruders roam the Frozen North.*

Tom opened his eyes. "There are trespassers in the North," he told Elenna. "And that can only mean one thing."

Elenna nodded and smiled grimly. "I'm going to need my fur cloak!" she said. "Kensa and Jeng had better watch out!"

THE BROKEN STAR

Tom and Elenna hurried along the palace's vaulted corridors until they reached Jeng's former throne room. Sunlight streamed through the huge stained glass windows that covered one end of the chamber, casting bright patterns across the floor. The spicy scent of incense hung heavy in the air. Irina and

Freya stood together beside Jeng's velvet-padded throne, deep in conversation. They looked up as Tom and Elenna entered.

"How did you get on with our guest?" Freya asked. Her face was pinched with worry, but the dark smudges beneath her eyes had gone.

Tom smiled, relieved to see his mother looking so strong after Kensa's poisoning. "Elenna's a born interrogator," he said. "Sanpao told her everything. Apparently, Kensa and Jeng are after a powerful artefact in the North. Something they call the 'star'?"

Irina's face drained of colour and she slumped into the cushioned throne behind her. "The ancient powers help us!" she said. She drew a long, trembling breath.

"So you know what this 'star' is?" Elenna asked.

"I'm afraid I do," Irina said. "I suspect Jeng is after the Broken Star – a star-shaped rock that fell from the sky long ago. It shattered into four shards when it landed – and it's believed to have landed here. Jengtor was built in the shape of a star to honour this gift from the sky. The event slipped from common memory into legend long ago. Only a chosen few still know the star is real." Irina took another deep breath and went on. "Unfortunately, Jeng is one of those few. And to make matters worse, he also knows each shard grants the bearer great power."

Tom felt a cold finger of fear trace his spine. "What power?" he asked.

Irina paused, her lips pressed tightly together. "The power to control the elements," she said.

Tom and Elenna exchanged a horrified glance. They knew only too well what Kensa could do with such power. Recently, the Evil Witch had almost plunged Avantia into eternal winter. "We have to find those shards before Kensa and Jeng get anywhere near them," Tom said.

Irina sighed. "Easier said than

done. Centuries ago, a Good Witch named Clara scattered the broken pieces, for the safety of Gwildor. Since that day, they have been guarded by four Beasts – Gryph, Thoron, Okko and Saurex. The Beasts are Good, but have never been tamed, and have not had many dealings with the people of this kingdom. They live in isolation, guarding their fragments fiercely."

Tom looked to Freya. "Mother – surely between us we could convince the Beasts to give up their treasures, so that we can keep them out of Jeng's hands?"

Freya shook her head, her dark eyes filled with regret. "There are still pirates looting all over Jengtor," she said. "With the emperor gone, it is my duty to lead the people against them. You and Elenna have to complete this Quest alone. But I must warn you – these Beasts have never known a Mistress or Master. It will not be easy to earn their trust."

Tom held his mother's troubled gaze, firm resolve building inside him. "We'll earn it," he said.

Freya's frown softened. "Kensa and Jeng have a head start on you. If they are willing to challenge ancient Beasts, they must have some powerful evil magic prepared."

Elenna swung her bow across her back. "We'd better get going, then," she said. "It will take days to reach the Frozen North on horseback." She stopped and shook her head. "We can't ride Angel and Star. They're not made for snow and ice. I don't think they'd survive the trip."

Irina smiled wearily. "Few animals could," she said, "which is where I can help." She crossed to Tom and bent, extending her hand and clicking her fingers. The purple jewel Tom had won from Sting the Scorpion Man freed itself from his belt and floated neatly into her palm.

Tom understood at once. The magic gem had once opened a doorway to lead him and Elenna out of Gorgonia.

"Can that stone open a magical path to the North?" he asked Irina.

"It will," she said, "once I have

made some minor adjustments.
Please stand back."

Tom and Elenna waited as Irina
cradled the purple stone in her
hand. The Good Witch rubbed her
thumb over the shiny surface and
chanted a few words. Soon, where
her thumb brushed the stone, the
surface started to shimmer. A thin
coil of violet smoke drifted up, as
if a tiny fire had been kindled. The
smoke spread, creating a swirling
cloud as tall as a man. Irina blew
gently into the smoke, and the
centre cleared, leaving an archway.
Tom heard Elenna gasp in wonder.
Through the opening, he could
see an icy valley filled with snow,

flanked by jagged mountains.
Craggy outcrops of rock and blue
glaciers dotted the snow, along with
patches of coarse yellow grass. Tom
recognised the landscape.

"Freeshor!" he said.

Irina handed the purple stone to Tom. He fitted it back into his belt. "Thank you," he said. "Your magic has saved us several days' hard riding. We should be right behind Kensa and Jeng."

Irina nodded. "But to succeed in this Quest, you will need more help." She lifted her hand to her lips, and blew into her fist. When she opened her fingers towards Tom, her palm was filled with what looked like glittering embers. A sweet smell, like spiced oranges, wafted up from the glowing fragments. "These are magical herbs," Irina said. "Eat them. Their power will keep you as warm as the thickest furs."

Tom and Elenna each took a pinch of herbs. They felt cool in Tom's fingers, but when he popped them into his mouth, they crackled and fizzed, giving off a fiery taste, like cinnamon. A gentle heat spread down his throat and into his belly as he swallowed.

"Wow!" Elenna said, fanning her face with her hand. "Let's go before we cook!"

Tom found he was suddenly sweltering. He lifted his hand in farewell to his mother. "We'll be back as soon as we can to help with those pirates," he said.

Freya smiled. "I'll handle things here. You just be careful. The fate of Gwildor depends on you and Elenna once again."

Irina stepped back to join her friend beside the throne. "I wish you luck on your Quest," she said.

Tom squared his shoulders, and peered out through the magical portal. The rocky grey and white landscape looked deserted. But somewhere on the frozen plains, Tom knew a fierce Beast waited – a

Beast he would have to challenge. And Jeng and Kensa were out there too, brewing up Evil he could only imagine. He took a deep breath and turned to Elenna.

"Ready?" he asked.

"Ready!"

They stepped together through the portal, into the freezing wastelands of the North.

OLD FRIENDS AND OLDER ENEMIES

An icy gust slammed into Tom's body, snatching the breath from his throat. He braced himself against the gale and squinted in the wind. He was standing on a narrow, rocky path with rugged grassland on either side – dry tussocks, furred with frost, half buried in snow. Tom took a step, and felt the treacherous slip of ice beneath his boots. He glanced back. Elenna was just behind him. Beyond her, the grey landscape merged into the blue-white glow of glaciers in the distance. The portal to the palace was gone.

"Which way?" Elenna said, shouting over the wind.

"We'll follow the road north, since that's where Kensa's headed," Tom called back. He scanned the horizon. There was nothing to be seen of the sun but a pink smudge shrouded in cloud, sinking into a line of jagged mountains. The light was fading fast from the short arctic day.

"That way's west," he said, pointing

towards the sunset. "We need to follow the road uphill."

They turned and set off at a steady pace. Ice creaked under their boots and the wind whipped at their clothes as they trudged onwards. Soon, as the last embers of sunlight

bled from the darkening sky, fat
flakes of snow started to drift down
around them, as thick as swarming
flies.

The flakes landed on Tom's lashes
and found their way inside his
clothes. Cold meltwater trickled
down his skin. The wind seemed to
come from every direction at once,
buffeting his body and smothering
the path. With nothing to see but
swirling greyness, it was hard to
tell if they were still heading the
right way.

Tom stopped and stared into the
blizzard, trying to find a landmark.
Elenna slammed into his back,
almost throwing him over.

"Sorry," she said, her voice snatched at by the wind. "I didn't see you!"

"This is hopeless!" Tom said, squinting into the gloom. Suddenly, he spotted something that made his nerves prickle – a tall, pale blue shape trudging towards them through the snow. Tom gripped the hilt of his sword, but as the figure drew closer, he recognised the broad, angular outline of Koldo the Arctic Warrior. Tom lifted his hand in greeting.

"Koldo!" he shouted.

The Good Beast stepped out of the blizzard and dipped his head to Tom and Elenna. His ice-blue face

was creased into a furrowed frown.
He hefted the jagged ice club from
his shoulder, and leaned on it, like a
staff.

You came quickly, Koldo said.

Tom pressed his fingers to his red jewel. *Kensa and Jeng are looking for a shard of the Broken Star that is hidden here in the North,* he said, communicating with the Beast through his mind. *Can you lead us to them?*

Koldo nodded curtly, bent his massive shoulders into the wind, and trudged away. Tom and Elenna followed.

Before long, the whirling flakes began to thin. The wind dropped. Tom was finally able to look about him and take in the frozen landscape. Huge glaciers jutted from the snow all around them.

The dark clouds above parted, revealing glimpses of teal-blue sky, scattered with stars. In the distance, Tom could make out slim trails of pale smoke drifting upwards. He pointed.

"Freeshor," he said. He glanced at Koldo, expecting to see some flicker of emotion in the ice Beast's face. But if the arctic warrior was remembering the time he had been cruelly imprisoned there, surrounded by fire, he didn't show it. He led Tom and Elenna onwards between the towering glaciers to a steep road rutted with sled tracks.

They crested a ridge in the road and a broad horizon opened

up before them. Tom could see
the silhouetted huts of Freeshor,
squatting beneath their smoking
chimneys. Beyond them, the land
rose steeply. Towering over the
tiny village, a vast palace of ice
dominated the view. Its sharp towers
jutted into the evening sky. The
windows were black and empty,
showing no sign of life within.

"It looks deserted," Elenna said.
But there was something about
the cold and lonely palace that set
Tom's spine tingling. He called on
the power of his golden helmet
and gazed towards it, scanning the
courtyard with his enhanced vision.
He quickly spotted two sets of

footprints: one narrow, and one large and square.

"Someone's in there," Tom said. "My guess is Kensa and Jeng are using the palace as their base."

"We'd better go and see what they're up to," Elenna said.

Tom, Elenna and Koldo followed a steep, winding road until they reached the palace courtyard. The two sets of prints led them straight to the palace door.

"Let's take a look," Tom said, pushing the heavy slab of ice. It opened with a creak. Tom and Elenna stepped into a narrow, arched corridor. Koldo stooped to enter behind them.

Tom scanned the passage, his breath forming white puffs in the still air. Gritty snow had been driven into the hallway by the wind. The footsteps carried onwards to an archway at the end, then stopped. Through the archway, Tom could see a long cathedral-like chamber, with a high, vaulted ceiling supported by columns of ice either side. Moonlight filtered down through the ceiling, casting blue shadows across the ground. At the far end of the chamber, raised on a platform carved with stars, sat a glittering throne of ice. There was no sign of whoever had made the footprints.

Elenna shot Tom a puzzled look.

Tom put his finger to his lips and quietly slipped his sword from its sheath. They crept along the passage.

"Be ready," Tom hissed to Koldo and Elenna. He lifted his sword, drew a deep breath, and stepped through the arch.

"'Ready' won't help you this time!" A harsh, female voice echoed down from above.

Kensa! Tom looked up to see the Evil Witch suspended near the ceiling with Jeng at her side. The pair were surrounded by a globe of sparking blue energy. Kensa's green eyes flashed with triumph as they met Tom's. A trap! She lifted her Lightning Staff.

Crack! A blinding bolt of energy
lashed from Kensa's staff and
smashed into the base of a pillar.

The pillar exploded into a shower of ice. Tom and Elenna sprang back as the cascade hit the ground, skittering outwards in a burst of glittering shards. The violent shockwave of the impact threw Tom from his feet. Trembling ice met his outstretched hands. Elenna hit the ground beside him. The crack and ping of splitting ice filled the air, along with the cackle of Kensa's laughter.

Tom scrambled up, keeping his balance low until the quaking stopped. He glanced up, but Kensa and Jeng had vanished. A loud, ominous creak echoed through the chamber. Tom felt an answering shudder run across the ground. The

whole room seemed to tremble.
Elenna grabbed his sleeve, and
pointed. One of the columns that
held up the ceiling was leaning,
crazed with jagged white cracks.

Tom ran his eyes along the rest of the columns and his mouth went dry. All were laced with crooked fractures. A tremendous roar, like an avalanche, erupted all around them. The first column burst apart, turning the air white with spitting ice.

FIRE AND ICE

Tom tugged Elenna towards him
and threw up his shield against the
shattered ice falling around them.
Through the shuddering, ice-filled
chaos, Tom saw Koldo lunge past.
The arctic warrior dived towards
the doorway and used his massive
shoulders to brace the trembling
arch. His fierce blue eyes met Tom's.

Run! Koldo's voice shouted in Tom's mind. *Before you are crushed.*

"We have to get out, Tom!" Elenna cried. Tom glanced at Koldo, hunched beneath the archway, the flat planes of his ice face scrunched together with effort.

"We can't just leave him!" Tom cried.

A loud, grating creak echoed from the ice ceiling above them. "We don't have a choice if we want to save the kingdom!" Elenna cried.

Tom saw that she was right. Beyond Koldo, fragments of ice were already raining down inside the passage. If they didn't leave now, they never would.

Tom dashed across the room
with Elenna at his side, shards of
ice pummelling his shield. They
ducked beneath the protective arch

of Koldo's arm, into the passage. Their feet clattered over slippery rubble as they raced towards the distant arch of sky. The trembling grew stronger. The ground shook with such violence Tom could feel it rumbling in his chest. He glanced back to see Koldo, straining beneath the archway, his blue eyes burning brightly. A great section of ceiling buckled and fell. The Good Beast vanished in a torrent of white. *No!* Tom's feet flew over the heaving ground even as his heart clenched with fear for his friend. His breath came in ragged gaps, burning his chest.

At last, he and Elenna burst from

the passageway into the palace
courtyard. The sound of splintering
ice rose to a deafening roar as they
raced across the frozen ground.
There was a thunderous crash
behind them, followed by brittle
a sigh, like wind through snowy
branches. Then silence. Tom and
Elenna skidded on a few more paces,
then turned.

"Koldo!" Elenna gasped, her
eyes wide with horror. The palace
had been reduced to a mound of
blue-white rubble, glittering in
the starlight. Tom put his hand
to the red jewel in his belt, cold
dread welling inside him. The Good
Beast's frustration hit him like a fist,

driving away his fear. Tom smiled.

"Koldo's not hurt," Tom told Elenna. "But he is trapped. It will take him some time to dig himself out, but he'll be fine."

Elenna heaved a sigh of relief. "Then we'll have to find Kensa and Jeng alone," she said. "And it looks like they went that way." She pointed towards two lines of familiar footprints, leading away from the remains of the palace.

Tom and Elenna followed the tracks, the rising moon casting their shadows before them like slender giants. A bitter wind blasted Tom's cheeks and whipped up eddies of snow. But, under his tunic, he was as warm as if he had been wearing a heavy fur cloak. He felt a rush of gratitude to Irina for her protective spell. The cold was one enemy they wouldn't need to fight on this Quest.

Tom's attention was suddenly drawn to a line of flickering orange points appearing from between two glaciers ahead. He gripped the hilt of his sword, his skin prickling. *Fire!*

The orange lights bobbed as they drew closer, and soon Tom could see the bulky black outlines of people huddled beneath them, holding torches.

"Isn't that Dylar?" Elenna said, pointing to a stocky, hunched form at the head of the procession. Tom could just make out the chief tribesman's craggy face, thrown into shadow by his torch. Dylar had mistakenly held Koldo captive on Tom's last Quest to Freeshor, and Tom remembered him well.

"Greetings, Dylar!" Tom called, as the village elder drew close.

Dylar held up his staff, and the procession stopped behind him. The stocky, weather-beaten chief held his torch to one side and peered at Tom. His lined face spread into a broad smile under his fur hood. "Tom!" he cried. "And Elenna!" Dylar strode forward and clapped Tom on the shoulder, then clasped

Elenna warmly by the hand. "It's good to see you two again," he said. He ran a puzzled frown over their clothes and let out a bark of laughter. "You'd be the only two warriors wild enough to come to the

North without cloaks. And it's just like our wise Emperor Jeng to send us help before we ask."

Tom and Elenna exchanged an uneasy glance. "What do you mean?" Tom asked.

"Evil is brewing in the North," Dylar said. "A giant bird Beast rages across the land. We were heading to Jengtor for help."

"Then you haven't heard the news," Elenna said. "Jeng isn't the emperor any more. He betrayed his people, and turned to Evil."

Dylar stepped back, his eyes wide with shock. At that moment, a screeching voice filled Tom's mind. It was so loud, the pain forced him to his knees.

Who dares to steal the star?

Tom clutched his head and forced his gaze upwards. A blaze of shining white streaked towards him through the night. As it hurtled closer, Tom made out the sleek lines of a giant bird, broad wings thrown back behind it, and talons outstretched like glinting knives.

GRYPH ATTACKS

Who dares challenge me? The Beast's shrieking voice filled Tom's mind. He couldn't move – he couldn't even think beyond the pain. But he could see every terrifying detail of the giant falcon plunging towards him. He watched in helpless horror as her white form blotted out the night. Her dark eyes flashed with menace and her cruel talons opened wide.

BOOF! Elenna cannoned into Tom's shoulder, throwing him

sideways. Gryph's talons struck
the ground, showering Tom with
splintered ice. A shriek of rage filled
the air, then the *swoosh* of beating
wings. Tom's reeling senses cleared
and he scrambled to his feet. Dylar
and his people were scrambling for
shelter as Gryph swooped skywards.
Her huge wings glimmered in the
moonlight. Tom gasped. Each white
wing feather was tipped with a
crystal blade, far finer than the
sharpest steel.

Tom put his hand to the red jewel
in his belt, and focused his strength
of will. *Gryph!* Tom called with
his mind. The giant bird levelled,
hovering above them. Her broad

wings beat the icy air and her eyes
fixed on Tom.

*I am Tom, Avantia's Master of the
Beasts,* Tom told her. *I come here as
a friend.*

Gryph let out a long, keening cry
that sounded to Tom like mocking
laughter. Her voice blasted through
his mind. *I am Gryph the Feathered
Fiend. I protect the white shard of
the Broken Star. Try to steal it and
you shall perish!*

Tom held the bird's sharp gaze.
*There are people planning to steal
it, and they are close by. But I ask
you to give it to me freely, so I
can keep it from falling into their
hands!*

Puny boy! Gryph's voice raged like a blizzard in Tom's mind. *I will not give up the shard to one so weak!* She threw back her wings and dived, plummeting like a falling dagger aimed straight towards Tom's heart.

"Elenna, run!" Tom cried. Elenna darted back to stand beside Dylar and his people beneath the overhang of a glacier. Tom lifted his sword and stood his ground. The orange light from the villagers' torches flickered across Gryph's wingtips as she sped towards him. Something else glimmered too, buried deep in the feathers of her right wing. A long silver-white

crystal, tapering to a wicked point.
The shard!

At the last possible moment, Tom
dived into a roll. Behind him, he
heard the shriek of splintered ice as

Gryph's talons hit the ground. He leapt to his feet and rounded on her, brandishing his sword.

Gryph's eyes flashed. One crystal-tipped wing sliced at Tom's chest.

He blocked it with the flat of his sword, feeling the impact jolt along his arm. The Beast's other wing whistled through the air, its deadly tips lashing towards him. Tom leapt back and lifted his shield, bracing himself.

Smash! The blow lifted him off his feet. He landed hard on his back in the snow. Gryph opened her wings and lunged.

Suddenly, an arrow whizzed through the freezing air, parting the feathers on the Beast's vast head.

Gryph's long neck whipped around, and her keen eyes rested on Elenna. Tom took the chance his friend had given him. As Elenna

circled the Beast, a second arrow
aimed at the falcon's ribs, Tom
scrambled to his feet. He ducked
beneath the Beast's right wing and
swiped upwards with his sword,
aiming at the pale shard lodged
between her feathers.

Gryph danced back, snatching her
wing out of reach with a squawk.
Her vast head snapped around and
her curved beak slashed at Tom's
face. Tom threw up his shield.

Crash! The power of Gryph's
blow tore the shield from his
grip. He staggered back, but kept
his balance, holding his sword
before him. Tom swallowed hard,
steeling himself. Gryph opened

her long, curved beak and let out a
tremendous screech, her icy breath
slamming against Tom and freezing
the air in his chest. His sword arm

burned with the ferocious cold. He gasped in horror as a skin of frost spread across his hand and encased his sleeve. He tried to flex his elbow, but his whole arm was frozen stiff.

Gryph lifted her wing and swept its crystal tips towards him. Tom leapt back out of reach but, as he landed, the heel of his boot snagged on something hidden in the snow and he tumbled over. Gryph beat her wings once and was on him, her grey beak lashing at his face.

A DEADLY
EMBRACE

Tom heard a twang. The falcon's
head jerked up, her serrated beak
missing Tom's cheek by less than
a finger's breadth. She let out a
terrible shriek of rage. Tom could
feel the searing cold of it burning
the skin of his face. He could see the
shaft of Elenna's arrow buried deep

in the feathers of Gryph's wing.

The great bird shook herself. Her powerful wings beat the air, pinning Tom to the ground with the force of a hurricane. Then she wheeled into the sky.

Tom staggered clumsily to his feet, his sword arm as numb and useless as wood. Elenna raced to his side. "Are you all right?" she asked.

"Thanks to you," Tom said.

"But your arm…" Elenna reached out to touch his hand. When her finger met Tom's white, frost-coated skin, she snatched it away with a yelp. Tom tried to hold back the panic welling inside him. He hadn't felt her touch at all.

"We need to warm that up!" Elenna said, turning to Dylar and his tribe. They were huddled against the glacier, watching from the shadows beneath their torches.

"I need fire, quickly," she said.

A tall, bearded man stepped forwards and thrust his torch towards her. More of the tribe joined him, craning their necks to see as Elenna dropped her bow and grabbed the torch. She knelt, holding it well below Tom's frozen arm. Immediately, Tom felt the skin of his hand and arm start to tingle with a maddening, itching pain. He gritted his teeth to stop himself pulling away. The tingling and

burning got worse as the ice on his
sleeve melted and the blood returned
to his limb, turning his fingers from
bloodless white to a raw, meaty red.

Finally, he found he could flex his hand and bend his elbow.

"How does it feel?" Elenna asked.

"It hurts," Tom said, "which means it will mend." Then a glimpse of movement above Elenna drove all thought of pain from his mind. A white form was streaking through the night, with the speed of a falling star.

"Take cover!" Tom shouted to the tribespeople gathered around him. Mothers and fathers snatched up their children and ran for the scant shelter of the glacier. Gryph plummeted downwards, her crystal-tipped wings shining silver in the moonlight. Tom braced himself, sword and shield raised as she swooped low. The Beast's eyes sparked with what looked like amusement as they fell on Tom and Elenna. Then she opened her beak and let out another icy gust.

Tom bundled into Elenna, throwing her out of the path of the deadly cold. They tumbled together through the snow, the sound of Gryph's wingbeats all around them. As Tom scrambled to his feet, he saw Gryph bearing down on the townsfolk cowering against the glacier.

I have to get Gryph away from those people!

"Gryph! Over here!" he cried. The Beast's massive head swung around, and her angry gaze met his. Tom turned and ran as fast as he could, away from the terrified townsfolk. He could hear Elenna's footsteps behind him. The light of her torch cast wavering shadows ahead.

The snow banked steeply, and soon they were clambering over bare rock. Tom reached the crest of the rise, then froze, his heart hammering. He flung out an arm to stop Elenna. The ground dropped away suddenly at their feet, in a near vertical snowy slope scattered with sharp points of rock. A gust of wind whooshed past, almost throwing Tom from the ledge. He braced himself, and turned to see the edge of Gryph's razor-wing swiping towards them. "Elenna, get down!" Tom cried. Elenna ducked and scrambled away as Tom threw up his sword.

Clang! Blade met blade with a
force that rang along Tom's arm.
His stomach leapt as he teetered
backwards, arms flung out, trying
to find his balance. Gryph beat her

massive wings, hovering in the air, her fierce eyes fixed on Tom. Then her deadly claws snapped open and slashed towards his chest.

Tom blocked Gryph's talons with the flat of his sword, bracing his feet against the ground. He somehow kept his balance, and lifted his sword once more. Gryph landed on the slope below him, her talons clutching the rock. Her eyes glittered coldly as she flung back her vast white wings. Then she swept them forwards suddenly, the crystal tips cutting the air, folding around Tom's body in a deadly embrace.

Before the wings could close,

Tom bent his knees and leapt. With no other choice, he threw himself backwards off the ledge.

He fell through empty space, his muscles clenched against the impact to come. Gryph's wings smashed together, filling the air with a ringing, crystal note.

Thud! The impact as Tom hit the ground drove the breath from his lungs. Pain blossomed in his shoulder. He tucked himself into a roll, sharp rock biting his back as he tumbled. Finally, he slid to a stop at the base of the slope. The steep side of the snowy rock face rose above him, at least five times his height.

Gryph glared down from the top,

her wings spread wide. Beside her,
a slender figure bearing a blazing
torch stood at the crest of the rise.
Elenna! Gryph dipped her head
and dived, her sharp beak slicing
towards Tom. At the same moment,

Elenna bent her knees and leapt.

Tom stared in wonder as his friend
landed squarely on the falcon's
wing, then lunged, waving her
flaming torch in front of the Beast's
eyes. Gryph squawked and changed

course in an instant, angling sharply upwards. A harsh wind battered Tom as she swept over his head.

Tom scrambled to his feet to see Gryph climbing through the starry sky. The flame of Elenna's torch and the dark shape of her body were silhouetted against the Beast's white wing. Gryph levelled then dived, turning a sharp loop before climbing again. *She's trying to throw Elenna off!*

Gryph swooped low and Tom saw Elenna clinging on for her life. Her eyes were narrowed against the wind and her hair was plastered to her head. Her mouth was a thin, grim line of terror. As Tom watched, she lowered her torch, and touched the flaming tip to Gryph's feathers.

A shudder of agony ran through the great bird's powerful frame. Gryph opened her beak and let out a screech of anguish and fury that echoed through the night. The falcon banked sharply, tucking her wings against her body, and dived like an arrow fired from the sky. The flame from Elenna's torch trailed behind her.

Tom's body went tight and cold. *If Elenna hits the ground at that speed, she'll die!*

GUARDIAN OF THE SHARD

Tom stared, breathless with horror as Gryph plummeted towards the rocky ground, taking Elenna with her. He could see the terror in his friend's face, but he could do nothing to help her. *She has to make it!* Gasps of fear rose from Dylar's tribe as Gryph sped onwards, her shadow clear and crisp on the moonlit rock below.

Almost too late, Elenna flung herself free of the diving bird. Her legs windmilled in the air as she flew over bone-shattering rock. Tom tensed, watching his friend plunge to the ground…

Elenna landed in a tight roll and

disappeared into a thickly piled
drift of snow, her torch blinking
out in a puff of smoke. Tom set off
running towards the drift that hid
his friend. Above, Gryph screeched
and pulled out of her dive, swooping
low over the jagged rock towards
the snow where Elenna lay buried.

Tom raced against the shadow of
the Beast. *I have to reach Elenna
first!* He glanced up to see Gryph's
long talons scything towards the
drift. Tom called on the power of his
golden boots and leapt towards the
bird, slashing his sword at Gryph's
talons. The giant bird flapped
her wings and veered skywards,
snatching her curved claws out

of reach. Tom landed shin-deep in snow, and fell to his knees. He peered into the drift, terrified of what he would find.

Elenna lay curled on her side, her knees pulled up to her chest and her arms thrown over her head.

"Elenna! Are you hurt?" Tom cried, gently shaking her huddled form.

Elenna uncurled slowly and sat up, blinking. Her hair and lashes were white with snow. Her face was paler still.

"I don't think so," she said, flexing her shoulders gingerly.

"Then come quickly!" Tom held out his hand. "We have to take cover!"

Elenna gripped Tom's hand, and he tugged her up. They set off, half running, half skidding, towards the icy overhang where Dylar and his people clustered. When they reached the shadow of the glacier, Tom threw his back against the wall, and looked up. Gryph was a white arrowhead in the starry sky, climbing and swooping in majestic arcs.

Tom looked down at Elenna, crouched at his side.

"This is the bit where you normally come up with the plan," she said weakly.

Tom gnawed at his lip, following the path of the bird with his eyes.

He could see her watching him, as
if she was daring him to attack.
"There has to be a way of defeating
her," he said.

A deep rumble echoed down
from the mountains. Tom tensed,
listening hard.

"An avalanche?" Elenna asked, her
eyes wide with fear.

Tom peered out from behind the
overhang, towards the ruins of the
ice palace. The glinting form of
Koldo stood tall against the night
sky. As Tom watched, the arctic
warrior lifted a huge chunk of
glittering ice over his head with
both hands, leaned back, and hurled
it towards Gryph.

The bird's dark eyes flashed
and her wings tipped, altering her
course. The block of ice sailed past
her. It hit the ground and shattered,
tiny pieces skittering in all

directions. The villagers let out cries of alarm and pressed even closer to the glacier wall.

Koldo flung another missile, but Gryph swerved and dodged with the grace and speed that only a falcon could master.

"She's too fast," Elenna said. "And Koldo would never hurt a Good Beast, anyway."

"No," Tom said, feeling a rush of gratitude for the giant. "But he's bought me time to come up with that plan. And I think I've got an idea."

Tom turned towards the tribespeople gathered beside them. Dylar was at the front of the group, his broad arms circling a pair of fur-hooded children. Tom stepped towards him. "Do you have a rope?" he asked.

Dylar nodded. "I can do better than that." He gently pushed the children aside and let his pack fall from his shoulders. The old chief stooped and drew a long metal chain from his bag. It clinked as he handed it to Tom. The metal felt newly oiled and surprisingly light.

"That's Ice Iron," Dylar said. "It was smelted from ore that can only be found in the caves of Freeshor. We use chains like this to pull timbers through the snowy ground. It doesn't rust, and it's almost

impossible to break."

Tom ran the smooth, cold links
through his fingers, and smiled.
"It sounds like just what I need."
He quickly tied two loose knots
in the chain and made a loop,
then passed the slack end through

the opening he'd made.

"A lasso! Good thinking," Dylar said.

Tom looked out from beneath the overhang. Gryph was bearing down on Koldo, a raging storm of flapping wings and tearing claws. The arctic warrior swung his jagged club, swiping at her wings, forcing her back. But, as he drew his club back for another strike, Gryph jabbed her sharp, curved beak at his chest, landing a powerful blow. Koldo staggered and fell, his massive club flying from his hand. Gryph hung in the air above him, letting out a victorious screech. Then she turned a swift loop and dived back towards the overhang where Tom waited, watching for the right moment.

Now! Tom stepped from the shelter of the overhang into the falcon's path. Gryph's eyes flashed with triumph. She spread her wings, slowing her flight, and reached her talons towards the ground. She was so close, Tom could see every detail of her razor claws and hooked beak. He tightened his grip on the chain.

The Beast shot him a scornful look, then swept her crystal-tipped wings together, slicing at his face.

Tom channelled the power of his golden boots and leapt up through the night air. He soared over Gryph's deadly wings, landing in a crouch behind her. Tom spun, lifted his lasso and started to swing.

Gryph turned and stabbed at him with the sharp tip of her beak. This was just what Tom had wanted. He let his lasso fly. The metal loop flashed through the air and dropped neatly around her frost-feathered neck. Tom leapt back and pulled on the chain with all his strength. The loop tightened around Gryph's throat, biting deep into the feathers. The giant bird reared and bucked, straining against the chain. Tom called on the strength of his magical breastplate and dug his heels into the ground. His arms shook and his muscles burned, but he didn't loosen his grip. Gryph jerked her powerful neck from side to side. Tom gritted his teeth and tugged harder, pulling

his lasso tight. The giant bird's eyes shone with fury. Her beak snapped open, letting out a blast of freezing air. Even the herb-embers in Tom's stomach weren't enough. He kept the lasso taut with one hand, and flung up his shield with the other, using the power of Nanook's bell to protect himself from the deadly cold. Then he gave the chain in his hand one last, sharp tug.

Gryph's head jerked forwards. She let out a strangled squawk. Her legs buckled and her feathered chest hit the snowy ground. Her wings sank down around her, spread wide like two white fans.

Tom took up the slack in his chain

and stepped towards her. He could see the feathers of her back moving with each exhausted breath. She lifted her head, watching Tom with her steady, black-eyed gaze. Tom put his free hand to the red jewel in his belt.

The Beast's voice filled his mind, but this time it was calm, and edged with a grudging respect. *Son of Gwildor...* she said. *I am vanquished.*

THE POWER OF THE STAR

Tom held tight to the chain lasso
wrapped about Gryph's neck, ready
to pull hard at the slightest sign of
a struggle. The villagers stayed
silent beneath the overhang, wide-
eyed in the darkness. High on the
ruins of the ice palace, Koldo
stood poised, a chunk of ice

clasped between his hands.

Release me, Son of Gwildor, Gryph said, speaking into Tom's mind. *I will do the people no harm.*

Tom held the Beast's gaze for a long moment, staring into the depths of her proud gaze, until he was sure she spoke the truth. Then he loosened his grip on the lasso.

Tom stepped forwards. He took hold of the loop of metal around Gryph's neck, and pulled it over her head.

Gryph stood and shook out her ruffled feathers. She opened her right wing, and extended the tip towards Tom. The crystal blades shimmered coldly in the moonlight, turning to feathers of the purest white. Buried deep in the snowy feathers, the jagged white shard gleamed. Tom took a breath to calm his racing heart, stepped forwards, and tugged it free.

A tremendous cheer erupted behind him from the tribe. Dylar and Elenna stepped from beneath the overhang to Tom's side. More fur-clad figures soon crowded forwards, keeping their distance from Gryph.

Son of Gwildor, Gryph said again. *You have proved yourself worthy to be guardian of the shard. But you must do so three more times. The next shard is north-west of here, in a place called Vareen. Should it fall into your enemy's hands, the power to destroy the realm will be theirs.*

The Good Beast's words filled Tom with resolve, steeling his body and mind. He spoke aloud to the

Beast. "I'll repair the star," he said. "And I'll use it to defeat Gwildor's enemies, once and for all!"

Another cheer went up from the tribespeople. High on his icy lookout, even Koldo lifted his fist. Gryph spread her massive wings and leapt into the sky. Tom watched her climb until she was nothing but a pale speck among the stars. Then he turned to Dylar.

"Elenna and I must leave at once. We have another shard to find. You should be able to return to your village in safety now."

Dylar grinned. "We are in your debt again. If you are ever in need of food or shelter, or an iron chain, you know where to find us." He turned to his people, and lifted his staff. "It's time to go home!" he said.

The villagers cheered and crowded around him. Dylar started off, leading his people into the night. Before long, their line of torches passed between two glaciers and vanished.

Tom looked up at the remains of the ice palace, where Koldo still stood, watching. The ice giant slowly nodded in farewell, then turned. A moment later, he was gone.

"Let's go," Tom said to Elenna.

"Not so fast!" a familiar female voice snarled behind them.

Tom and Elenna spun. Two fur-
coated, hooded forms still crouched
in the shadow of the glacier. They

were dressed like the villagers of Freeshor, but their eyes were as cold as flint. They threw back their hoods and sprang to their feet. With a jolt of fury, Tom recognised Kensa and Jeng.

"Get the shard! I'll see to the girl!" Kensa screamed at Jeng, lunging towards Elenna.

The muscular emperor bundled towards Tom, fists flying. Tom kicked out, throwing Jeng over backwards. Kensa shoved Elenna down into the snow, then swiped at Tom with her staff. Tom ducked, but Kensa changed direction mid-swing and brought the staff down hard on the back of his head.

Tom hit the ground and rolled onto his back, white specks crowding his vision. Kensa was standing over him, her lighting staff raised.

"Don't!" Elenna cried. She had her bow drawn, an arrow aimed at Kensa's skull. But as Tom watched, Jeng slammed into Elenna's back, sending her sprawling.

Kensa grinned down at him. "Thank you for doing all the hard work!" she said. "But now the shard is mine!" She jabbed the tip of her staff hard into Tom's chest, pinning him to the ground, and reached for the shard in his hand.

No! Tom felt ice-cold rage searing

through his body. A powerful surge
of energy flowed along his arm.
The white shard in his fist glowed a
bright silver. Kensa's eyes went wide
with fear and she leapt away from
Tom. A blast of energy exploded
from the shard. It spread out in an
arc, hitting Kensa and throwing her

from her feet. Jeng cried out
in pain and fell backwards,
landing with a thud. Even Elenna
yelped and curled into a ball as the
icy energy flowed past her. Then the
blast was gone.

I did that! Tom realised, staring at
the pale crystal in his hand.

The sound of Kensa scrambling to her feet focused his attention. The witch's green eyes were wild with anger. She struck her lightning staff on the rocky ground, releasing a plume of thick black fog.

Tom leapt up and stared into the murky fug, but he couldn't see a thing. When the smoke finally cleared, Kensa and Jeng were gone. Only Elenna remained, still balled tightly on the ground.

Tom ran to her side. "Are you all right?" he asked.

Elenna slowly uncurled and sat up. A violent shiver ran through her body. "I've never known a wind so cold!" she said.

Tom ran his thumb along
the sharp edge of the shard,
remembering the feeling of its
fierce, cold energy flowing through
him. He nodded grimly. "The blast

came from the shard," he said. "It's a powerful weapon."

Elenna swallowed hard and shook her head. "We can't let Kensa get her hands on a power like that."

"You're right," Tom said. "While there's blood in my veins, I'll do whatever I can to keep it out of the villains' hands – and keep the people of Gwildor safe."

CONGRATULATIONS, YOU HAVE COMPLETED THIS QUEST!

At the end of each chapter you were awarded a special gold coin.
The QUEST in this book was worth an amazing 8 coins.

Look at the Beast Quest totem picture inside the back cover of this book to see how far you've come in your journey to become

MASTER OF THE BEASTS.

The more books you read, the more coins you will collect!

Do you want your own
Beast Quest Totem?
1. Cut out and collect the coin below
2. Go to the Beast Quest website
3. Download and print out your totem
4. Add your coin to the totem
www.beastquest.co.uk/totem

Don't miss the next exciting Beast Quest book, THORON THE LIVING STORM!

Read on for a sneak peek...

RACE TO THE BORDERLANDS

Tom could sense the fear spreading through the Freeshor tribespeople. Men, women and children stood with shoulders hunched as if they could make themselves smaller and disappear into the icy landscape.

"Nowhere is safe," Dylar, the tribe's leader murmured, pulling his thick furs tighter around his body. "Not while Emperor Jeng and that witch Kensa are on the loose."

"Then they must be stopped!" another tribesman said.

A young woman gave a bitter laugh. "They have magic on their side and we have nothing." Her younger siblings clung to her skirts. "It's impossible."

"Nothing is impossible." Tom strode into the centre of the tribespeople, his gaze sweeping over their worried faces. "I will stop them. I promise."

An older tribesman, bent double

with age, stepped forward. "How?" he asked, his hand clenched on the walking stick he held.

Tom's fingers went to the pouch hanging from his belt and released the white shard that he'd won on his last Quest. He held it up for all the tribespeople to see. "I proved myself in combat and won this from Gryph the Arctic Falcon," he said. "This fragment of a Broken Star has the power to summon freezing air. Kensa and Jeng wanted it to strengthen their dark magic, but I stopped them." He placed the shard back in its pouch. "There are three more shards to find, but I will stop the emperor and witch from getting them." His hand dropped to the hilt of his sword. "By the time my Quest is finished, the witch and the treacherous emperor will pose no threat to the Freeshor people."

There were cheers from the tribespeople and Elenna smiled at him proudly, coming to stand at his side. She didn't need to say it, but Tom knew that she would be with him on every step of this Quest. They both understood how powerful the shards were. If Kensa and Jeng got even one of the star fragments then the whole kingdom would be doomed.

As the tribe's cheers began to quieten, Dylar strode forward. "Tell

me where you're both heading now.
It would be my honour to help you."

"Koldo the Artic Warrior told us
that we must go north-west," Tom
explained. "To a place called Vareen."

Dylar grimaced. "Vareen is in the
borderlands. I've never been there,
but I've heard it is a barren, desolate
place from which travellers rarely
return."

"Great," Elenna murmured, an
eyebrow arched. "We love Quests
with an easy start."

Dylar gave a smile of approval.
"You are clearly brave, but you'll still
need transportation. The borderlands
are many leagues from here." He put
two fingers in his mouth and gave a

sharp whistle.

Almost immediately, a tribesperson arrived with a wooden sledge by his side. The sledge was pulled by four muscular Gwildorian huskies. Their fur was a russet colour, the same shade of a sunset in Avantia, and their eyes were almost white.

"They're beautiful." Elenna knelt down and stroked each huskie in turn. Tom could tell she was missing Silver, her pet wolf.

"Beautiful, but unpredictable," Dylar warned. "Still, they will get you to Vareen."

Tom shook his head in protest. "Your offer is very kind. But it would not be fair to leave the dogs on the

edge of this new territory while
Elenna and I continue our Quest."

"Gwildorian huskies have an
amazing sense of direction," Dylar

reassured him. "They always find their way home." He shook Tom's hand. "Good luck. My kingdom's future relies on you."

Tom nodded once and then climbed up onto the sledge next to Elenna.

Let the Quest begin, he thought to himself.

They set off, moving northwards through the icy fields. The blades of grass were frozen solid and they crackled and snapped underfoot as the Gwildorian huskies raced across the landscape.

The sledge skimmed swiftly across the plains and Tom's hands tightened on the reins. He told himself that it was to control the direction of the huskies and not because he was scared of the breakneck speed they were going. He turned and saw that Elenna was holding the reins just as tightly as him. Her cheeks were red from the wind that lashed them, and she was concentrating hard on keeping her balance as they turned a sharp corner.

Her eyes suddenly widened and Tom whipped round to look up ahead. They were hurtling towards a vast, frozen lake!

"The ice!" Elenna yelled over the wind that was howling past them. "What if it doesn't take our weight?"

Tom yanked on the reins, urging the huskies to stop at the edge of the lake, but they paid him no attention. They leapt straight onto the ice and skidded forwards with yelps of excitement. Beneath their barks, Tom heard the ice of the frozen lake creak in protest as it got used to the weight of the sledge. But it held.

The huskies surged forward and their yelps faded as they focused on the route ahead. That's when Tom heard it...

A cracking noise that could mean only one thing.

The ice is giving way.

Read *Thoron the Living Storm* to find out what happens next!

FIGHT THE BEASTS,
FEAR THE MAGIC

Are you a BEAST QUEST mega fan?
Do you want to know about all the latest news,
competitions and books before anyone else?

Then join our Quest Club!

Visit the BEAST QUEST website
and sign up today!

www.beastquest.co.uk

Discover the new Beast Quest mobile game from

Available free on iOS and Android

 amazon.com

Guide Tom on his Quest to free the Good Beasts of Avantia from Malvel's evil spells.

Battle the Beasts, defeat the minions, unearth the secrets and collect rewards as you journey through the Kingdom of Avantia.

DOWNLOAD THE APP TO BEGIN THE ADVENTURE NOW!

Not final artwork. Produced and created by Miniclip SA and Beast Quest Ltd. All rights reserved.